Chakra

Tecniche straordinarie
per emanare energia,
potenziare l'aura
e armonizzare i chakra

di Ananta Del Greco

ISBN:1547228202
ISBN-13:9781547228201

The Knocking

by

Maggie Holman

Run Jump Jive

Also by Maggie Holman:
'The Wishing Sisters'
'Footprints in the Snow'

*

'The Knocking' © Maggie Holman 2017

Maggie Holman asserts the moral right to be
identified as the author of this work.
ISBN 978-90-820089-3-7

Cover design by Nik @ Book Beaver with
original woodcut from 1607

In memory of the victims of the Great
Flood

I

I arrived at Severn Cottage in the middle of a hot July afternoon. The cottage was very old, made of local stone, exactly as my Mum's friend had described it. It stood on the side of the road, with a small enclosed garden behind, and looked out across its namesake, the wide and sweeping River Severn. I parked up on the gravelled area to the side, searched in my bag for the keys and walked round to the front door, which was made of ancient heavy wood. It creaked and groaned as I turned the key and gave it a push.

Inside, I discovered a patchwork of worn flagstones under my feet and original beams above my head. I walked along the hallway into a cosy living room with a dining table, a well-loved sofa and a wood burner inside the inglenook fireplace. Further on, the cheerful kitchen mixed traditional cupboards and shelving with convenient mod cons and a narrow wooden staircase beckoned me upstairs. As I climbed the bent, worn stairs, they creaked and groaned their way through my ascent. On the first floor, I found a narrow landing running parallel with the hallway below. Two windows looked out onto the steep hill behind the cottage. When I peeped out, I noticed a single tree at the summit, standing like a sentry on guard. Even though it was the middle of July, the tree looked dead, a bare black silhouette against the summer sky. No cheerful summer foliage adorned its branches. Instead, they pointed into the clouds like sinister, warning fingers.

I carried on and explored a pretty, tiled bathroom and two bedrooms. The first bedroom had a large window which looked out over the river. The second had two small windows looking back onto the hillside. Both bedrooms contained the usual holiday-let furniture. Here and there, framed prints of local views decorated the walls, and in both rooms, a disused coal fire grate was now a display for vases of dried flowers. I decided to sleep in the first bedroom. I liked the view of the river, and the tree on the hill already made me feel uncomfortable. I didn't want it to be the first thing I saw when I woke up.

My inspection complete, I went back to my car. I pulled out my suitcase and a carrier bag of groceries. Next, I brought in all my study items; a laptop, a printer and a box containing text books, notebooks, folded maps and my digital camera. I set everything out on the dining table, which was going to be my temporary office for the next month. Finally, I went out one last time to lock the car.

When I came back into the cottage, I splashed through some water just inside the front door. A small puddle filled the worn centre of one of the flagstones which hadn't been there while I'd been going in and out. I bent down and dipped my fingers in it. It felt slimy, and smelt dank and muddy. I cleaned it up with an old rag from under the kitchen sink and watched for a moment, but no more water appeared.

Later that afternoon, I drove back into Awre. I'd driven through the village on my way in and it was like going back in time; a few terraced houses, some quaint cottages, a war memorial, a village shop, a church and a single pub, the White Horse Inn. I parked in the pub car park and went inside. Just like the cottage, the lounge had a traditional feel to it; horse brasses hung on the stone fireplace and a display of copper pots and pans filled one corner. A large painting of the view across the river hung on the wall. The room was empty, except for a girl about my own age who was cleaning glasses behind the bar at the far end.

"Hello," she said, smiling as I approached. "What can I get you?"

"Half a lager, please. And do you do food?"

"Certainly do. Here you go."

She passed me a menu and I ordered a cheese sandwich while she poured my drink.

"You passing through?" she

asked.

"No, no. I'm visiting. I just drove up from London today. My Mum's friend owns a holiday cottage, down by the river. I've never been up this way before and I've come to stay for a month. I've been told it's really quiet."

"Certainly is. The whole place is quiet. Dead might be a better description. I never met anyone who wanted to stay around here for very long before. It's quite boring most of the time. So, you're staying at Severn Cottage, then?"

"Yes. Do you know it?"

"Sometimes I jog past it on my morning run. It doesn't take long to get back to the village on the riverside path. Cuts the corner off. Nice walk if you fancy it."

"Thanks. I'll remember that."

When a young man in an apron brought my sandwich, I pulled myself up onto a bar stool and began to eat.

"Is the cottage nice?"

"Yes, it is. It's quite cosy, just what you'd expect from a holiday let."

"And you're staying there on your own?"

"Yes. Why?"

"Isn't it a bit remote?"

"I'm not afraid of a bit of 'remote'. I'm looking forward to it, after the crazy-busy of London."

The girl looked a bit wistful.

"I've never been to London. I've never really been anywhere. It's nice to chat to someone my own age even round here! Most people are either old age pensioners or middle-aged farmers."

We both laughed.

"What's your name?" she asked next.

"Megan."

"I'm Ginny. I hope you enjoy your stay."

"Thanks. Actually, I'm not just here on holiday, and I've come to ask you a favour," I pulled a handful of leaflets from my bag. "I'm here to do some interviews for a university report and I was wondering if I could leave these on the bar?"

Ginny shrugged her shoulders.

"OK with me, and I'm sure the manager won't mind. What sort of interviews?"

"I have to write a paper about people's attitudes to risk. I'm studying psychology, see, at UCL. My Mum's friend – the one who owns the cottage – told me about a huge flood that happened in this area, and I thought it would be interesting to use it as the basis of my paper, interview some locals about the risk of another flood."

Ginny picked up one of my leaflets and studied it.

"They had some really bad floods in Gloucester and Tewkesbury a few years back, but not so much round here," she commented.

"This flood was a long time ago, back in 1607. It's known as the Great Flood. A huge wave came up the river and more than two thousand people drowned. Now scientists think the wave could have been a tsunami."

Ginny shook her head, incredulous.

"A tsunami? Here, on the Severn? I never heard that story."

"It's not a story. There are public accounts and church records from the time, and recently, scientists have gathered geological and geographical evidence."

"But how could there have been a tsunami here? That's the sort of thing you see happening on the news in other countries, not in England."

"They think there was an underwater earthquake in the Atlantic. It created enough energy to cause the huge wave."

"Wow. You certainly sound like a student!" Ginny laughed.

"Sorry, I wasn't trying to sound like a smarty pants. I just read up on it a lot before I decided to come. Anyway, the point of my paper is to find out if local people know about the Great Flood, and if they're worried about the possibility of another wave that big."

"And here's me saying nothing exciting ever happens round here! Well, leave the leaflets with me and I'll pass them around."

"Thanks. I appreciate it."

"You're welcome."

II

The solitary location of the cottage was perfect for studying and I quickly got into a routine. I started each day with a short jog along the river, then I sat at the dining table to work on my report. In the afternoons, I went out to take photos, check out local sources and find people to interview. I went to bed early, got up early and I slept soundly and undisturbed. Everything was going according to plan.

Only two things caused me any bother as I followed this routine. One was the uncomfortable feeling every time I caught sight of the lone tree up on the hill, and the other was the repeated appearance of the slimy puddle inside the front door. I continued to clean it up, but no matter what I did, it always came back. What was also strange was that if I waited for the puddle to appear, and watched the flagstones carefully, it never did. Whenever I turned my back, there it was! I e-mailed my Mum and asked if she could mention this problem to her friend. Perhaps there was a leak in the pipes under the floor?

*

Unfortunately, my peaceful routine didn't last forever. In the middle of the second week, I woke up, disturbed by a noise, a solitary 'click'. It sounded like the click of the old-fashioned latch on the bedroom door. The digital clock on the bedside table said one-thirty. I lay still in the darkness for a moment, waiting, then I leaned up on one elbow and turned on the bedside lamp. Everything looked the same, but the room *felt* different. I decided I'd been dreaming and was about to turn off the light and lie down again, when I heard a footstep outside the bedroom door.

This time I was alert in a second and sat up quickly. I listened to a quiet footstep, then another, and another. Someone was walking very slowly past my bedroom door. Moments later I heard the creaking of the stairs. The footsteps continued to move slowly. Whoever it was, they were trying to tread carefully, and I thought back to Ginny's question about me being on my own in this remote place. Surely no-one had broken into the cottage? I thought of my mobile phone, left downstairs on the dining table. I couldn't call the police, or anyone else. I was all alone. The footsteps stopped, and I pondered on what to do next; stay here in my room or go and investigate.

A set of hearth tools – poker, shovel and brush - hung on a frame beside the fireplace. I climbed out of bed, crept across to collect the poker and went over to the bedroom door. I lifted the latch slowly enough to avoid its same clicking noise. When I opened the door, and looked up and down the landing, there was no sign of life at all. I stood there, still wondering whether I'd imagined the footsteps, when, suddenly, someone ran along the hallway towards the front door.

The poker made a clattering noise as I dropped it on the floor and sank against the wall, my composure gone. I forced myself to breathe slowly. I told myself that whoever it was – hopefully just kids? – would run off if they knew I was aware of them, and so I called out in my bravest voice.

"Who's there?"

Silence, more silence and even more silence. After waiting an age, I picked up the poker and set off down the stairs. I walked through the cottage, turning on every light as I went. I checked every window, and then the back and front doors. They were all shut tight and locked. Nothing seemed amiss. I turned all the lights off again and sat on the sofa, my retrieved phone in my hand. I couldn't see how the intruder had got inside, but I was ready if they came back. I waited fifteen minutes, half an hour, and nothing happened. I went back to bed and lay on my side, wide awake and listening, but eventually I must have fallen asleep, because the next thing I knew I woke up to bright sunshine streaming through the curtains.

Ten minutes later I sat at the kitchen table, hugging a cup of coffee, and thought through what had happened during the night. If someone else told me they'd heard unexplained footsteps, my first response would be to assume they'd imagined it all, or dreamt it, something like that. Did I dream those footsteps outside my door? No, I rationalised. I was awake. Did I imagine them? Maybe. The brain plays tricks, I told myself, especially at night.

After breakfast, I cut up a sheet of printer paper into long, even strips. I went all around the ground floor of the cottage, systematically opened each window, folded a strip of paper over the top and shut it again. It was a trick my Dad taught me when I got a ground floor room in my first university halls. Now, if anyone opened a window when I wasn't at home, the paper would fall out and give away their entry. I would do the same to the back and front doors each night, before I went to bed.

III

I had an appointment that morning with a local farmer, a Mr Slater. I locked the front door and got into the car, resolving to put the weird footsteps out of my mind. I left Awre, drove back up the winding road towards Newnham and turned left into the entrance of Seven Oaks Farm. The farm was small, and I saw no signs of any oak trees that had given it its sturdy name. A brick-built farmhouse stood to one side and a few sheds and outhouses stood around a parking area in the middle, where two men were busy throwing straw bales into the back of a pick-up truck. I parked beside them, just as one of the men got into the pick-up, waved at me and drove off. The other man smiled at me.

"Mr Slater?" I asked.

"Yes. Please, call me Peter. Are you Megan?"

"I am. Hello."

He dusted his palms off on his jacket and we shook hands. He looked to be in his forties, a friendly giant, tall and stocky, with a ruddy complexion.

"Thanks for taking time to meet me."

"No problem. It was my Dad who saw your leaflet in the White Horse. He pops down most afternoons for a pint and tries to chat Ginny up."

I laughed.

"Anyway, come inside. I'll put the kettle on."

Peter made two mugs of coffee and put them on the kitchen table. We both sat down, and I took my laptop out of my bag.

"Are you enjoying your stay?" asked Peter.

"So far. The scenery is beautiful."

"It certainly is. Right, then. What do you want to ask me?"

"Well, first of all, how long have you lived in the area?"

"All my life. I've always lived on this farm. It's been in our family for six generations, since Matthew Slater bought it, back in 1834."

"And do you know about the Great Flood in 1607?"

"Of course. I think most people know about it."

"Do you know what happened?" I continued.

"It devastated the area. Washed whole farms and villages away. A good part of the population drowned, and some people think it might have been a tsunami."

"Ah, that was my next question. So, you already know that theory? What do you think?"

"I know it was a sudden powerful wave, and that's what a tsunami is like. People had no warning, no time to get away. I've seen a couple of documentaries on television and read up on the internet. I'm just interested in local history and that sort of thing."

"Do you know how the tsunami was caused?"

"Possibly an underwater earthquake. The water would've been high anyway, that time of year, and that only added to the problem. We always have to watch the spring tides round here."

"So, do you think there could be another tsunami?"

"Of course."

"Why?"

"Well, when there's been one underwater earthquake, there can always be another. If that happened with the same conditions as on the day of the Great Flood, we'll get another Great Flood, right?"

I typed furiously, keeping up with Peter's answers.

"So, does it worry you, living with the possibility of another tsunami?"

"Worry me? Well, being a farmer, I keep a constant eye on the weather forecasts - you have to - and I hope, in this day and age, we would get enough warning. They have plenty of technology!"

"Do you have anything in place here, in case of such a flood?"

"When you live near a river, flooding is always a risk. I've got a mate, another farmer, who's up on higher ground. We've got a plan together to move the cows if it looks like serious flooding is likely, and take them up to his place, but in the case of a fast wave without any advance warning, I guess no, personally I don't have a plan in place."

"Does that bother you?"

Peter paused.

"I suppose if it really bothered me, I wouldn't live here, would I? And, there are other, more realistic risks around here. I mean, some of the cars race along the A48 like lunatics. There's been loads of accidents recently, and a quiet farm like ours, just me and my Dad, well, we've been burgled a couple of times. The Great Flood happened four hundred years ago. I said there *could* be another tsunami, in principle, but if I'm honest, no, I suppose I don't really think it's likely."

I finished my typing.

"Does that help you with your research?"

"Yes," I replied, "very much, thanks."

"If we're done here, my Dad wanted to meet you. He's out the back."

"OK."

I followed Peter outside. Behind the house, an old man, also tall and stocky, was busy digging in a vegetable patch. He looked up, planted his spade in the ground and came to meet us.

"Dad, this is Megan."

"Hello," he said, reaching to shake my hand. "Jack Slater."

"Hello."

"You wanted to show Megan something, didn't you, Dad?"

"Yes. Follow me."

We walked along the back of the house and stopped at some large double doors in the nearest shed. Together, Peter and his father opened each door, pushing them wide. I gasped a little. Inside was a huge wooden boat. It wasn't a sailing boat. It had no masts. It had no engine either. It was a simple rowing boat, but its base was wide and its walls were higher than a usual rowing boat design.

"Built it myself, over thirty years ago," said Jack.

"Dad's not like me, Megan. He's not one of the complacent types, right, Dad? He's always thought there might be another Great Flood, and he's ready if it comes."

*

Back at the cottage, I decided on a run. I got changed and set off along the sunlit path. I concentrated on my breathing and my pace, as I ran on and on in an effort to escape my thoughts. Jack's boat had unsettled me, although I couldn't say why. I ran on a bit further than on my previous runs. The path lay closer to the edge of the river, twisting and winding alongside it like a faithful friend. Ginny was right; it was a nice route. I rounded a new bend and unexpectedly came across a wooden bench. Behind the bench, on the inland side, a wide marshy area was overgrown with reeds and bulrushes. It stretched all the way back towards the hillside. The bench was placed so that it looked towards the river, an ideal spot for passers-by to stop and take in the view. It seemed to beckon to me to sit and rest, so I did. I leaned back, stretched my arms along the warmth of the wood and surveyed the scene in front of me. The river was calm and flowed smoothly by. A few twigs and leaves and the occasional duck floated along in the swirling current. On the opposite bank, the flat fields stretched away into the distance. The trees and fences grew smaller and smaller, stretching away in pop-up layers until they disappeared over the horizon.

No-one had passed me on the path. No canoes or boats putt-putted by. I couldn't even hear any birds singing. I was just getting my breath back and thinking about how quiet it was, when the peaceful moment was broken by the sound of giggling behind me. I turned quickly, but all I could see were the reeds, blowing from side to side in the gentle breeze. The giggling had sounded young, girlish. I was sure I heard two different voices. I bent down and tried to peer through the tangle of leaves and reed stems, fully expecting to find a couple of mischievous teenagers hiding from me, but no-one was there.

I watched the reeds a little while longer, then I turned back around. Immediately there came the sound of more laughter. This time it seemed to come from the left of me, but when I looked in that direction, more laughter came from in front of me. How could that be? The   laughter continued, behind me again, then to the right, left, right. I stood up and turned in all directions, this way and that, until I felt dizzy from trying to keep up. Wherever I looked, no-one was there. I tried to step down into the reeds to explore further, but my trainers threatened to sink into the soft, waterlogged ground.

"Hello?" I called out to the invisible voices. "Who's there? Are you teasing me?"

The laughter stopped immediately. I waited, a little unnerved, but everything stayed silent. I turned around and ran quickly back to the cottage, where I found the puddle waiting for me.

IV

A few days later I went into the village at lunchtime, on my way to my next meeting. I had an appointment with two elderly sisters who'd apparently lived in the village since the Second World War. I found the address, the second in a row of four terraced houses, and rang the bell. The door opened just a crack. An elderly lady, white-haired and pale, looked up at me.

"Miss Noakes?" I said, putting on my best smile. "We spoke on the phone."

"Oh yes. Are you Miss Wallace?"

"Yes. Please, call me Megan. I have my ID if you need it. Is it still convenient for me to have a chat with you?"

Miss Noakes closed the door. I heard her unfasten a chain and pull back a bolt. She opened the door again and stepped back.

"Yes, of course. Do come in. I'm Margaret. Hello. My sister Emily is sitting out in the back. Please, come this way."

I followed Margaret through the house and into the conservatory. Another elderly lady was sitting in the corner, facing the sunny garden.

"Emily. Wake up, dear. The young lady's here. The one who wants to ask us about the flood. I've got some tea and biscuits ready for us all. You do drink tea? I'll just go and get it."

Both the sisters were old, but Emily was clearly the elder of the two. She opened one eye and squinted at me. Her gnarled hands, twisted with arthritis, gripped tightly onto a woollen blanket which lay across her knees. She eyed me warily and I smiled uncomfortably back, pleased when Margaret returned with refreshments on a tray.

"Now," she said, as she passed me a cup of tea, "what exactly do you want to ask us?"

I opened my laptop and got ready to type.

"Well, I'm doing a survey and have a list of questions. My first question is, how long have you lived in Awre?"

"Oh, years. Let's see," Margaret paused, working something out. "We came in 1949, that's sixty-eight years ago. I was seventeen and Emily was twenty-one."

"That is a long time!"

"Oh, yes. We were in London throughout the war, Emily, Mother and I. Us girls were evacuated for a little while, but we missed Mother so much, we cried and cried until we were allowed to come home. Our father was in the army from 1941 and he was horribly wounded in France at the D-Day landings. He needed constant care when he first came home and he never completely recovered. Mother wanted to bring him somewhere quiet. They came here on a short break, decided they wanted to stay and us girls came along to help. After Father passed away, then Mother too, well, we just stayed on."

"I'm sorry."

"Why? No need to apologise. We love it here, don't we, Emily?"

"OK. My next question is, do you know about the Great Flood, the one that happened in this area in 1607?"

"Yes, we do, don't we, Emily?" Margaret addressed her sister again.

"And can you tell me exactly what you know?"

"Lots of people drowned, on both sides of the river. I'm not sure how many, but I've read that whole villages were just washed away. It must have been terrible."

"So, do you know how the flood was caused?"

"Just the weather, I suppose. A winter storm surge, wasn't it? The Severn's well known for it. Something about the wind and the rain and the

Spring tides coming together in a certain way."

"And did you know that there's scientific evidence that the flood was more than a flood, that it might have been a tsunami?"

"Really? How could that happen, here I mean?"

"Some scientists think there was an underwater earthquake in the Atlantic that pushed the wave upriver."

"Well, I never!" Margaret was surprised. "Emily, what do you think of that?"

Emily stared into the garden, her expression fixed.

"So," I continued, "My next question is, have you and Emily considered that a flood of such a huge scale might happen again, that those circumstances might come together in the same way?"

"Not really, no. I mean, we've been here so long and we've never been flooded in all that time. Some of the roads around here are liable to a bit of flooding. A lot of this area is reclaimed land, you know, but our house has always been alright. I think over the years things have been done to keep the water at bay, and these days I think we're all a bit more aware, what with television and all. 1607 was ever such a long time ago, you know."

"And do you think that local people are generally aware that such a flood could happen again?"

"No, I don't think so. I mean, I think a lot of people *know* about the 1607 flood, but I really don't think everyone expects it to happen again. I'm not sure if there's an emergency plan organised by the local council or anything like that, and we'd certainly know if there was. I go to all the public meetings!"

"Have you, yourselves, here at home, have you got anything in place if there is such a flood?"

Margaret paused.

"Well, no. Do you think we should? I mean, is there *really* a risk, after all these years?"

I suddenly wanted to end this interview. I didn't want to frighten these two old ladies. I smiled painfully. Margaret smiled back and leaned over to pat my hand.

"Well, you know, Megan, we lived through the Blitz and survived. Father was hurt on D-Day but he still lasted quite a long time. Emily and I, we're not afraid of a bit of water, are we, Em? Us Noakes's are tough! And anyway, I suppose with all this technology they use, they'll see it coming and tell us - won't they?"

I smiled again, less painfully.

"I'm sure they would."

I closed my laptop. As I finished my tea, I listened to Margaret's stories about how Awre had changed over the years. It was clear the sisters didn't get many visitors and she was enjoying the attention.

"Well, Margaret," I said, packing up my things, "I'm afraid I do have to go. Thanks for the tea and for helping me with my questions."

"It was nice to meet you, wasn't it, Emily? You're welcome to call in any time if you're going by."

"Thanks."

Just as Margaret and I stood up, the sound of footsteps crossed the floor above us. I looked up quickly at the ceiling. Margaret didn't react at all.

"What was that?" I asked.

The old lady shrugged.

"It happens now and then. Emily and I aren't concerned. We like to think it's Mother, or Father, or the both of them, hanging around in the house they loved. If it's not them, no matter. No need to be afraid of any previous residents!"

I said goodbye to Emily and followed Margaret along the hall.

"But this," she sounded exasperated, "*this* is something new. I just don't know what to do about it."

We stood together, staring at a small puddle which was seeping through the carpet by the front door.

"That was dry when you arrived. It's been going on for a couple of weeks.

I clean it up and it comes right back. Makes the carpet smell terrible."

"That's really strange, because the same thing is happening in the cottage where I'm staying. Did you get anyone to look at it?"

"Oh, yes. Our regular plumber came out. Couldn't find anything wrong."

v

That night, I was woken by a sound outside my room. Once again, the clock said one-thirty. I lay in bed, wide awake. I wasn't imagining anything. I could definitely hear footsteps. I listened to them, frozen in my spot, not moving a muscle, as they passed my bedroom door and went along the landing towards the second bedroom. I reached for my phone on the bedside table and called 999.

"Which service do you require?" said a woman's voice.

"The police. I think someone has broken into the cottage where I'm staying. I'm on my own."

The woman took the address and some brief directions.

"There's a car on its way. Stay on the phone and stay in your room until they arrive."

I clutched the phone tightly and listened as the footsteps passed my room again and I heard the creaking of the stairs. Okay, so, whoever it was, they weren't planning on coming into my bedroom. Silence filled the cottage again. I got up, threw on some clothes and crept to the window. A few minutes later I saw a pair of car headlights in the distance. I watched the police car approach and park on the side of the road. Two policemen got out and walked towards the front door. The sight of them gave me confidence.

"They're here," I said to the voice on the other end of the phone, and I hung up. I set off down the stairs and went straight to the front door to let them in.

"Hello, Miss Wallace. I'm PC Matthews. This is PC Johnson."

PC Johnson immediately began to search through the cottage, turning on the lights as he went, while I told PC Matthews about the footsteps I'd heard, and how it was the second time this had happened. He wrote everything down in his notebook just as PC Johnson returned.

"What're the papers for?"

"Something my Dad taught me, to show where someone got in."

"Right. OK, come and see."

We walked through the living room and the kitchen, examined every window and the back door.

All the papers were intact.

PC Matthews put his notebook away.

"Well, everything looks OK. There's no signs of a forced entry. You're sure you heard footsteps?"

"I'm sure."

"Old cottage like this, probably makes all sorts of strange noises, especially at night."

So, they didn't believe me.

"Is there anything else we can do? Can we give you a lift to stay with a friend?"

"No, thank you. I'm fine. I don't really know anyone here. I've come to stay while I do some university work."

"Well, everything looks safe for tonight. Call again if you have any more worries."

"I will. Thank you."

They got back into their car and drove off into the night. Sleeping seemed out of the question now. I made a cup of coffee and sat down at the dining table. I sat there for a long time, thinking. The footsteps had followed the same route on the two occasions I'd heard them, and now it was clear that no-one had got into the cottage. I took out a sheet of paper and began to write.

'A reappearing puddle,' I wrote first, then 'hearing laughter outside in the reeds, footsteps in the cottage, trip-papers intact, footsteps and a puddle at the Noakes' home as well.'

I paused then continued to write.

'Megan Wallace, you don't believe in ghosts. You *cannot* believe in ghosts. You're training to be a psychologist. You're supposed to look at everything from a rational, scientific point of view.'

I paused again, read what I'd written, sipped my coffee and wrote:

'Something to think about: *why* don't you believe in ghosts? Or – *should* you believe in ghosts?'

I think of myself as a level-headed sort of person. I've never been one for strange fancies about 'other worldly' things, but I had to admit that something strange seemed to be going on. I'd been more afraid that a real-life intruder had got into the cottage, and now that it was clear that hadn't happened, I was intrigued. How could a few footsteps cause me any harm? Perhaps it would be useful to keep track of these strange events, rather than ignore them. I decided to search online for any documented evidence about 'supernatural sightings at the sites of large scale catastrophes'. All this thinking made me tired after all. I went back to bed and slept soundly.

VI

Two days later, I was sitting at the dining table in the afternoon sunlight, typing up some   interview notes. A quiet rat-a-tat-tat came from the direction of the front door. I opened the door and discovered Ginny, out of breath, holding a cardboard cake box from the village shop.

"Cream cakes," she said, grinning, "to go with that cup of tea. I just jogged along the river and didn't drop them once. Honest!"

I laughed.

"Perfect timing for me to have a break. Come on in."

Ginny followed me into the kitchen, sat down at the table, opened the box and started to munch on a chocolate eclair. She looked around.

"Nice place," she commented. "I never saw inside before. Quaint."

"I like it," I said, pulling mugs and tea bags from the cupboard while the kettle boiled. "Sugar? Milk?"

"Just a bit milk, thanks. So, how's your research going?"

"OK, actually. I have to get at least fifty interviews done, to make the required sample. I've done eleven face-to-face interviews so far, I've got eight lined up in the coming week and fourteen people have used the online link on my leaflet."

"You can interview me if you like – I've been known to take lots of risks! - but not today. I have to start work at three and I'm not in 'interview mood'."

"Thanks. That would be helpful – a young person's perspective. Everyone I've met so far is over forty."

"Do people round here know about that big flood? I've never heard anyone mention it in the pub. Is it a real threat?"

"Could be. In one sense, for example, there's a threat just because if it happened once, it can happen again."

"The flood you told me about *was* four hundred years ago."

"I know, but there are other factors to consider."

"Such as?"

"Environmental issues, like the changing infrastructure of the planet, global warming and the general rise in water levels."

"I wish I was clever enough to go to university," Ginny teased.

"What makes you think you're not?"

Ginny shrugged her shoulders and attacked another cream cake.

"Anyway," I went on, "there are also social infrastructure issues. For example, the rivers don't get dredged anymore because we use roads for transportation, and that makes the rivers too shallow to cope with rising water levels. That was part of the problem in Gloucester and Tewkesbury in 2007."

"I remember. My brother helped to pull out a load of cars that got stuck along the bottom road. So, how many people died? In 1607, I mean."

"The records say over two thousand. The flood water covered about two hundred square miles along the Bristol Channel estuary. Not many people knew how to swim in those days."

I hunted around in a pile of papers on the table and pulled out an aerial map.

"See here? The bits coloured pink are the flooded areas in 1607."

"Including here. Look, here we are in Awre. If the village was flooded, then so was this cottage. It's so close to the river."

Ginny sipped her tea.

"It's really sad," she continued. "They didn't know it was coming and they didn't have time to get away."

"No."

I watched her. She'd gone quiet and looked uncomfortable.

"What's wrong?"

"Megan," she whispered, "don't you feel like you're being *watched*?"

I paused before I spoke, deciding how to reply.

"Why do you ask?"

She turned around and looked towards the hallway.

"It's just I had the distinct feeling that someone was behind me, standing over there in the doorway, while we were talking."

She paused. I looked across at the doorway.

"Just kidding!" she suddenly called out, slamming her hand on the table in her excitement. I jumped and then we both laughed.

"Had you going there!" she said.

"You did. You had me worried for a....."

I didn't get to finish my sentence. A loud crash from above made us both jump. Ginny stopped laughing. We looked at each other in silence.

"What was that?" she whispered.

"I dunno. Let's go and look."

"Really? Then you go first."

I walked tentatively up each creaking step of the staircase, with Ginny close behind.

"Maybe I left a window open and the wind slammed it shut," I remarked as I opened and closed first the bathroom door and my bedroom door. Nothing looked any different. In the second bedroom, we found the source of the noise. A watercolour print, which usually hung on the wall in between the two windows, was lying face down on the wooden floor. Tiny shards of glass made a rectangular pattern around its edge. The string on the back of the picture frame was intact. We both stood in the doorway and stared at the mess.

"So that's what made us jump," said Ginny. "Probably the nail fell out."

She walked past me and strode confidently into the room.

"Careful," I warned. "I'll go and see if there's a dust pan and brush downstairs."

A few minutes later we were brushing up the glass.

"The nail's still in the wall," said Ginny, "See?"

I joined her.

"Hmmm. Very strange."

"Freaky, if you ask me, that happening just when I was teasing you."

I picked up the picture, lay it on its back on the bed and proceeded to ease out the rest of the broken glass. Ginny inspected the nail a bit longer and then she looked out of each window.

"Megan, come and look at this."

I joined her at the first window and looked at some writing which was scratched into the wall, above the top of the window frame. *'We thank thee Lorde for giving us the Sayving Tree to sayve us from the fludde.'*

"Look at the other window," Ginny said next.

I walked to the other window and read: *'But we must looke on it with sadnesse for the reste of our dayes.'*

"What's the Saving Tree?"

"That tree up on the hill there," I pointed. "A few of the people I spoke to mentioned it, said it's always been called the Saving Tree but they didn't know why. It's had that name as long as anyone can remember."

"Maybe it uproots itself, marches down and helps us all in times of need, like those trees in Lord of the Rings. I saw the movie."

"Maybe," I replied. "Personally, I think it's creepy. I wonder how long this writing's been there, and who wrote it?"

We both stared at the words again. Suddenly Ginny looked at her watch.

"Oh, my Lord, I have to dash and get ready for work. Hey, there's a blues band on at the pub on Sunday evening. Only local guys but they're pretty good. It's my night off and I'll be going along. Why don't you take some time out from all this lonely studying, come along and meet my friends?"

"Thanks. I might just do that."

Downstairs, I waved to Ginny as she set off back along the riverside. I dumped the broken glass in the bin, then I locked the cottage and set off up the hill. The going was steeper than I'd expected and it took me a while to get to the top, all the time keeping the Saving Tree in my sights. Up close, it was much bigger than I'd expected. I walked around its wide trunk. The bark was broken and crumbling. It came away in my hands when I pulled at it. It definitely looked dead. There was no sign of leaves or new shoots anywhere, just old gnarled branches which must have twisted and turned their way upwards a long time ago, and then come to a halt, frozen in their creepy position, pointing towards the sky. What happened to it for it to get into this state, I wondered? I leaned against the trunk and stared at the cottage below, the river flowing by, the village a little further on. I looked up at the tree again.

"Why does everyone call you the Saving Tree?" I whispered.

I took a few photos and set off down the hill. As I walked away, I had a feeling I was being watched. I quickly turned back round, but of course no-one was there.

VII

I decided it was time to add a local historian to my list of contacts. Next morning, I searched online. There were a handful of local people offering historical services. The website of one in particular, a Bill Buckmaster, claimed to have extensive knowledge of the history of the River Severn. I dialled his number.

"Hello?"

"Mr Buckmaster? My name is Megan Wallace. I got your number from your website."

"Hello, Megan. How can I help you?"

We chatted for a few minutes. I explained briefly that I was staying at Severn Cottage and wanted to know a bit more about its history, and if he knew anything about the Saving Tree on the hill. He asked if I had time to meet him later that day, and to my surprise, he wanted us to meet at the entrance to the churchyard in Awre.

At two-thirty, I walked along the riverside and was the first to arrive outside the churchyard gate. A few minutes later, a battered old Fiat pulled up and parked on the side of the road. An elderly man got out, grey-haired and slightly built, wearing an old tweed jacket. He smiled as he walked across to join me.

"Megan?" he said, "I'm Bill. Hello. Well, then. Let's go inside."

The churchyard was ancient and overgrown. Huge trees reached upwards and blew in the breeze. A plague of wanton ivy attacked everything in its path, creating a blanket of green over grave, ground and tree. The headstones we passed were very old, cracked and leaning, their dedications weather-worn and hidden by moss.

"So, you're interested in knowing a bit more about Severn Cottage."

"Yes. I've been there a couple of weeks. It's full of," I paused, "character, and I wondered if you could tell me anything about its history."

"And aren't you wondering why we met in the churchyard?"

"Of course."

"This is where you'll find the most important information about your cottage."

He pointed to the far corner of the churchyard, where several headstones were leaning up against the boundary wall.

"I want to show you something I think you'll find interesting, just over there."

Bill stepped off the main path and began to tread respectfully between the graves. I followed him and joined him in front of one of the headstones.

"The graves in this part of the cemetery are the oldest," Bill indicated, "Their plot marks are long gone, and their headstones have been placed up against the wall. Look here. Can you read this one?"

I leaned forward and peered more carefully. The lettering on the headstone was almost completely worn away.

"No," I had to admit, "I can't really make any of it out, except two numbers, I think, a 1, then a 6. Oh!" I exclaimed, "Is it 1600 and something? Are some of the graves really that old? And look, there's part of a name there, near the top. I think it looks like E..L..I but the whole name looks too short to be Elizabeth."

"It says Eliza," Bill replied. "This is the grave of two people, sisters called Eliza and Martha Littleton. I brought you a transcription I made a few years back, when the headstone was easier to read."

He passed me an old notebook, open at a particular page, and I read out loud:

'Here lies Eliza Littleton, aged
17 years, and her beloved sister
Martha Littleton, aged 15 years,
dearest daughters of Joshua and
Sarah Littleton, of the parish of
Awre, who drowned together in
the saving of their dear mother's
life on 30th January in the year of
our Lord 1607'

"Oh, they drowned in the Great
Flood!" I said, staring at the paper in my
hand. "How sad."

"Yes, and I've also got a
transcript of a pamphlet of the time,
which fills in the story a bit more."

I took the paper and read aloud
again:

'At midday on 30th January in the
year of our Lord 1607, Miss
Eliza Littleton was plucking
chickens in front of Severn
Cottage, which does lie close to
the river. Suddenly she ceased
her work and did hurry inside,

screaming in a great agitation
that a huge wave was coming
towards them. She did take her
younger sister, Miss Martha
Littleton, and her mother, Dame
Sarah Littleton, and they did run
as fast as they could up the hill
behind the cottage. The two
brave girls helped Dame Littleton
to climb up into the big tree at
the top. Dame Littleton did tell
us that the mighty wave travelled
at enormous speed towards her
daughters. Before they could
climb up beside her, the wave
caught the sisters both, and
washed them away. Dame
Littleton did say she could only
watch, screaming and praying to
God, as they disappeared under
the cruel water. Their bodies
were discovered three days later,
a full two miles down the river.
Master Joshua Littleton, the head
of the household, did not see the
tragic events unfold at his home.
He was already gone to Hereford

market with two of his five sons, James and Ishmael. His three other sons, Nathaniel, Thomas and Samuel, were working in the fields that day. When Master Littleton came home from Hereford, he was in great pain to discover that his two daughters and three sons were all drowned. The bodies of his sons are lost in the water. It was said to me, by the good people of Awre, that the Littleton family were honest, God-fearing folk, and that it is a great sadness for God to take so many of their children in this way.'

"I think this explains the writing on the wall back at the cottage," I mused out loud.

"What writing?"

"There's some writing carved into the wall above the two window frames in one of the bedrooms. It's a message about the Saving Tree."

"Really? Can I come and have a look at it some time?"

"Of course."

"Thank you, and Megan?"

Bill started to speak and then stopped himself.

"Yes?"

"Is anything…strange going on in the cottage?"

I looked at him for a moment.

"No. Why do you ask?"

"No matter. I was just wondering why you were so interested in finding out about its history."

"And you've been a big help. Thank you."

VIII

That night I couldn't sleep. I tossed and turned in the dark. When I heard the footsteps, I knew it was one-thirty before I looked at the clock. I sat up in bed, my quilt pulled up to my chin, and listened to the approaching steps. This time the footsteps were accompanied by a soft light, like a dim and flickering candle-light, which shone under the bottom of my bedroom door. A shadow broke the light under the doorway as the footsteps passed by and headed towards the second bedroom.

I didn't bother to move. I already knew that if I got up to look, no-one would be there. I already knew that if I checked downstairs, the trip-papers would be undisturbed. I listened to the footsteps come back along the landing. They stopped outside my bedroom door. The flickering light was at its brightest. I sat completely still, held my breath, felt my heart beat. I kept my eyes on the door latch, fully expecting it to move.

"They know I'm in here," I thought, "What are they waiting for?"

Nothing happened.

"Are you Eliza? Or Martha?" I finally called out, "Or are you both there? Are you still here in the house you were pulled from so cruelly?"

I waited. Silence.

"What do you want from me? Why are you trying to scare me? Do you want me to go away? Is it that simple? You don't want me in your home? Then tell me. Tell me what it is you want."

I watched the flickering light move away, become dim, heard the footsteps take their usual route down the creaking stairs. I sat up in the dark for a very long time.

*

Next morning, I got up and headed for the bathroom. When I opened the door, I stopped short. Across from my door, on the hallway wall, written in large letters, was a single word.

'leav'

I stared at it, touched it. It was written in slimy river mud. I went downstairs, found a piece of chalk in my box of odds and ends, went back to the landing and wrote in big letters 'Why?'.

"I'm not going to leave," I said out loud to the empty landing, "Why do you want me to leave? I don't mean you any harm. I came here to study and now I'm interested in you. The more you contact me, the more I want to understand."

I took a photo of the writing and made some notes, then I spent the rest of the day with my head in my books. Now and then I checked to see if I had a reply to my chalk question, but no more muddy writing appeared. Before I knew it, it was six o'clock in the evening. I was starving. I decided to kill two birds with one stone; eat at the White Horse and take up Ginny's invitation to watch the blues band, have some real life, human company for a couple of hours.

The lounge was already packed full of people when I arrived, and a big crowd was up dancing to a warm-up DJ. I fought my way to the bar to order steak pie and chips and a drink. I looked around. Ginny was waving frantically at me through the crowd, shouting something inaudible above the music. I waved back and made my way to the corner table which had been commandeered by Ginny and her friends.

"Suzi, Jack, Ollie, Joe," she called out, patting everyone on their heads in turn. "Guys, this is Megan, that clever student I told you about."

Ginny winked at me. I said hello as everyone moved around and offered me a chair.

"I don't really want to talk about my research tonight, Ginny," I shouted in her ear. "I've come to relax."

"What research?" she grinned back, tapping her hands on her knees in time to the music.

The evening wore on. I ate my meal and got up to dance a few times. At nine o'clock   the blues band came on. Ginny was right. They were good. People danced. They clapped and cheered, sang along. They seemed to know the band members by name. When the dance floor became more and more crowded I went to sit back down for a while. I sipped my drink and looked around. Everyone was having a really good time. From where I sat at the edge of the dance floor, I had a clear view towards the front door.

I watched the barman. He was busy wiping the floor just inside the door with a mop and squeezing the water into a bucket. He placed a plastic yellow cone that said, 'Wet Floor' on the mopped-up area and went back behind the bar. I got up and fought my way through the crowd.

"How've you got water on the floor there?" I shouted over the music.

The barman shrugged his shoulders.

"It started this morning. Every time I cleaned it up, it came back a while after. I thought it'd stopped but there it is again. It'd be just my luck for someone to slip, it's so busy tonight."

"Has that ever happened before?"

He shook his head.

"No, just today."

I went back to my seat. I'd had enough dancing and I sat through the rest of the show. Now and then, I saw the barman go back to mop up more water by the door. When the band finished at ten-thirty I said my goodbyes and set off back to the cottage. The night was clear, warm and still. The moon was bright. The stars made a twinkling canopy overhead. I walked along the riverside path and when I came to a familiar large rock, about halfway to the cottage, I sat down.

I shone my torch at the river. It slid slowly by, in and out of the beam, its surface black and sleek in the moonlight. The silence of the water, the hills, the sky, overwhelmed me. Something was going on, something which connected the whole area, not just Severn Cottage. I watched the calm water and tried to imagine what it had been like that morning, four hundred years ago, what it had felt like to be tossed and battered by a merciless wave, to have filthy, stagnant water invade

your mouth, your lungs and your life.
'Sorrow' was the word that came to me.
Heavy, unbearable sorrow. It bore down
on my shoulders, pressed me under its
emotional weight. Maybe it was the
beer, maybe I was tired, but I sat by the
water and cried.

IX

I checked the writing on the landing
when I got back to the cottage. The
muddy word was still there, dried out,
with my chalk question still unanswered.
I was surprised to find I was
disappointed. I felt wide awake and went
back downstairs to watch some TV.

    Later that night I woke up on the
sofa. It was pitch black and cold. The
television was still on, the volume turned
down low, and the news channel buzzed
quietly in the background. The moon
shone through the open curtains. By its
thin light, the clock above the fireplace
said one-thirty. I reached for the table

lamp and switched it on, stopped dead at what I saw. The wall behind the lamp was covered in words. I turned on the main light and looked around the room. Every spare piece of wall space was covered in words, written in the same thick mud as the writing upstairs. Messages in huge scrawling handwriting, mingled and repeated, travelling and jumbling over each other. Slowly I scanned the walls from left to right. *'get thee out,'* said one. *'Thy must be gone,'* said another. *'get thee from this huse,'* yet another, and *'leav now'*. By the time I followed the tumbling of words to the doorway, their message was clear and simple: *'get out'*

'get out' 'get out' 'get out' 'get out'

over and over again, in larger and larger letters until the message seemed to stretch to the ceiling. I stared at the writing. I couldn't move. I stood rooted to the spot and read the messages over and over.

Just then, all the lights went out. The television screen went black. At the same time, a loud banging made me jump. Someone knocked heavily on the front door. The sound echoed through the silent cottage. A pause, then more knocking, this time louder and faster. I set off to answer it, and the knocking continued as I walked. In the hallway, I stepped into water, ankle-deep, slimy and cold. Water was trickling under the front door. It gathered around my feet and began to spread across the flagstone floor, and all the time the knocking grew more and more frantic.

It stopped immediately when I opened the door. Outside, everything was quiet. When I looked out across the river, I gasped when I saw that it had burst its banks. The water had come right over the road and up to the cottage.

I splashed across the road to get a closer look, and as I did, I caught sight of movement out of the corner of my eye. I thought I saw a flash of a figure running across the road in the darkness. Just after, I thought I saw a second figure run by. I could have sworn they were dressed in long skirts, aprons and cloth caps, and that they hitched up their skirts as they ran.

I looked back to the river again, and suddenly everything began to happen quickly. At that moment the moon came fully out from behind the clouds. For a split second, I looked at a high black cliff, towering above everything in the moonlight, about two hundred meters down river, but then I remembered that there was no cliff there, that I should be looking at open fields. When I realised the cliff was moving, the terrible truth became clear. I was looking at a mountain of water, rolling and tumbling, surging and speeding, the normal path of the river forgotten as the land before it was eaten up by its immense width. At the wave's crest, strange sparks flashed and flickered, like a string of lanterns along a terrible horizon.

"Run!" screamed a woman's voice. I'm not sure I really heard the voice. I might have sensed it. It might even have been me who screamed at myself. It didn't matter. I turned, ran around the corner of the cottage, past my car, and headed towards the hill.

I woke up. It was biting cold. I couldn't feel my fingers or my toes. My whole body ached. I kept my eyes shut. I knew I was in the Saving Tree, curled up in a foetal-shape, my arms hugging my knees, at the corner point where the trunk split into its largest branches. At first, I couldn't bring myself to move. When I finally opened my eyes, a cloudy sunrise was just beginning to make its dull entry into the day. I stretched and began to sit up. When I saw the scene below the skyline, I sat bolt upright, fully awake.

Across the valley, as far as I could see, everything was under water. Severn Cottage was submerged up to its roof. The huge expanse of water was peppered here and there with the tops of the highest trees. The village of Awre had disappeared, replaced by a patchwork of upper floors and roofs. Part of the church spire pointed to the sky. Here and there I began to pick out movement, people in boats, travelling between the floating debris, and then a single helicopter flew across the horizon, looking completely out of place.

The edge of the flood water was about half way up the hill. Now I watched as a small dinghy approached and pulled itself up at the edge. Ginny was in it, sitting between two firemen.

"There she is!" I heard her shout.

Moments later, Ginny and one of the firemen stood beneath the tree.

"Oh, Megan. You're alright!" Ginny called up to me.

"Come on, Miss," said the fireman. "Let's get you down from there."

He climbed nimbly up into the tree, where I was clutching tightly onto one of the branches. He took my hands and tried to prise them away. At first, I resisted. It hurt to move, but eventually I climbed down with his support. Ginny hugged me with relief as the fireman wrapped me in a silver heat blanket.

"Just stand there for a minute," he said, "and get your legs back".

"The wave came," I said. I could barely speak, I was so shocked.

"Yes," Ginny replied. "The big wave, it came, just like you said it might."

"At one-thirty," I commented.

"Yes."

I looked at Ginny.

"Where were you, last night?"

"I decided to stop over at the pub. I woke up just in time and went up into the attic. I watched the wave. It was terrifying, Megan. I wrapped myself round one of the wooden beams and held tight. The force when it hit the building, I was sure it would wash us away, but the old pub held on."

I'd stopped listening. I was too busy thinking back to my last moments at the cottage.

"But how?" I interrupted. "*How* did you wake up?"

"Someone banged on the front door, frantic like. By the time I got to the window, the banging had stopped, and no-one was there, but then I saw the wave coming up the river and that's when I ran up to the attic. The pub's flooded up to the first floor. Everything's ruined, but at least I'm alive."

"Someone knocked on the cottage door."

"And everyone we've rescued so far has said they were woken up by a knocking," said the fireman.

"Really? Oh, the Noakes sisters? Martha and Emily?" I asked quickly. "Are they alright?"

"They're both fine," he replied.
"Are you feeling alright now? Come on,
let's get you down to the emergency
centre."

We walked slowly down the hill
and climbed into the waiting dinghy.

The fireman started up the engine
and we set off. Ginny sat next to me,
holding my hand. I stared in horror at the
devastation as we got closer to Awre.
Trees, broken fences and dead animals
floated past. I turned back just once to
look at the Saving Tree.

The rescue services, with help
from volunteers, were busy moving the
residents of Awre to higher ground.
Helicopters flew back and forth, and an
assortment of boats ferried people to the
water's edge. An emergency centre had
been opened in Newnham's primary
school, and many people in the
surrounding area opened their doors to
offer them a place to stay. Journalists
arrived, and television crews. The huge
area on either side of the River Severn,
which now lay underwater, found itself
beamed across the world, and survivors

told the same story over and over, how they were woken by a knocking, how someone came to warn them, or they would have drowned in their beds.

And what about me? No-one was trying to scare me off. I see that now. The puddles, the footsteps, the messages, the knocking; I was being warned, like everyone else, but for me there was more. I ran as fast as I could, slipping, stumbling, my chest pounding from the effort, but the truth is, I didn't escape the wave on my own.

Just as I knew I was failing, they came. I couldn't see them, but I sensed them. I couldn't see them, but I heard their laboured breathing and the rustle of their skirts as they began to run along on either side of me. I couldn't see them, but I felt them as they grabbed my hands in theirs and they pulled me up the hill.

Acknowledgements:
I am grateful to Jordan and David
Holman and Mitzi Waltz for reading
drafts of this story and giving
constructive advice.

The following sources were used during
my research:
en.wikipedia.org/wiki/Bristol_Channel_f
loods,_1607

http://www.bbc.co.uk/bristol/content/arti
cles/2007/01/30/flood_feature.shtml

https://www.surgewatch.org/historic-
events-the-british-channel-floods-of-
1607-2/

http://website.lineone.net/~mike.kohnsta
mm/flood/

http://forms2.rms.com/rs/729-DJX-
565/images/fl_1607_bristol_channel_flo
ods.pdf

https://issuu.com/lion7/docs/monmouths
hire

Printed in Poland
by Amazon Fulfillment
Poland Sp. z o.o., Wrocław